Belle

The Mysterious Message

This edition published by Parragon in 2012
Parragon
Queen Street House
4 Queen Street
Bath BA1 1HE, UK
www.parragon.com

ISBN 978-1-4454-9664-1
Printed in China

Belle

The Mysterious Message

By Kitty Richards
Illustrated by Studio IBOIX
and the Disney Storybook Artists

PaRragon

Bath • New York • Singapore • Hong Kong • Cologne • Delhi
Melbourne • Amsterdam • Johannesburg • Shenzhen

Chapter One

*I*t had been another lovely dinner at the Beast's castle. Although Belle did wonder if she'd ever get used to singing and dancing plates!

Belle sat at the long dining-room table. She held a cup of hot tea in her hands. The Beast had gone off to bed long ago. Most of the dishes and forks and knives and spoons had already washed up and put themselves away.

Belle took one last sip and set the teacup on the table. It spun around and started bouncing up and down. Its name was Chip. "Tell me the story of how you came to the castle again!" he begged.

Belle smiled at the eager little teacup. She had only been at the Beast's castle for a short while. But she had already told Chip the story four times. Or maybe it was five.

"I lived in a quiet village with my father, Maurice, not too far from here," Belle began. "We lived in a cozy cottage filled with his inventions. My village was a lovely place, but I didn't really fit in. Everyone thought I was . . ."

"Different!" Chip said.

"Chip," scolded his mother, a teapot named Mrs Potts. "Let Belle tell the story. It's impolite to interrupt!"

"It's all right, Mrs Potts," Belle said. She turned back to Chip. "Yes, they did think I was different. Mostly because I love books so much." Belle smiled. "Every time I started a new story, I was off on another adventure. But I still hoped for some real excitement in my life." She paused for a moment.

"And then your father got lost on his way to the fair . . ." Chip said.

"And then my father got lost on his way to the fair," Belle continued. "And when he didn't come home, I grew worried. So I set out to find him." She took a deep breath. No matter how many times she told the story, this part always upset her. "And I found him. He was locked in a cell in the castle tower."

Chip nodded. "And then the master showed up and you were scared!" he said.

"I *was* pretty scared," Belle admitted. By now she had gotten used to the Beast's fearsome appearance. But at first it had been pretty shocking.

"But then you were very brave and told the master you would switch places with your father!" Chip said.

"That's true. The Beast agreed and sent my father home," Belle replied.

"Then you found us!" Chip said excitedly. "And we're all enchanted! And you were very surprised!"

"Yes," Belle agreed. "I was very surprised to find a houseful of enchanted objects!"

Chip nodded wisely. "That's because an old beggar woman came to our house and asked for a place to stay," he explained. "But the master sent her away. She was really a beautiful sorceress. She turned the master into an ugly beast. And the rest of us into household objects as punishment." He turned to his mother. "It's not nice to be mean, right, Mama?"

"It's always best to be kind to everyone," said Mrs Potts briskly. "No matter what they may look like." She sighed. "Now off to the tub with you, Chip. It's almost bedtime."

"Aw, Mama," said Chip. But he could tell his mother meant business. "Okay," he said sadly. "See you tomorrow, Belle!" He hopped down the table toward the kitchen.

Mrs Potts took a deep breath. Belle did not know the whole story. The girl did not realize that there was a time limit on the sorceress's enchantment. There was a magical rose hidden in the West Wing of the Beast's castle. The Beast had to fall in love – and get the girl to love him. Then he would turn back into a handsome prince. And he had to do it before his twenty-first birthday. That's when the last petal would fall off the magical rose. If the Beast didn't fall in love, he and all the household objects would stay the way they were. Forever.

Mrs Potts was a cheerful, no-nonsense teapot. But she certainly did not want to be a piece of china for the rest of her life.

So Mrs Potts – and all the household objects in the castle – were hoping against hope that the master and Belle would fall in love. Then the spell would be broken. The two *were* becoming friendly. But it seemed nearly impossible that a beautiful girl like Belle would ever fall in love with an ugly beast.

"Good night. See you tomorrow," Belle said to Mrs Potts as she stood up.

Lumiere the candelabrum appeared at Belle's elbow. "Mademoiselle, may I be of service?" he asked with a deep bow.

"That would be lovely, Lumiere," Belle said. "I think I'd like to read a bit before bed. Let's go to the library."

"With pleasure," Lumiere replied.

Belle picked up the candelabrum and walked out into the hallway.

The Beast had allowed Belle to use his amazing library. There were more books in it than Belle had ever seen in her entire life. It was her dream come true.

She opened the doors to the huge room. Belle caught her breath as she saw shelf after shelf of books from floor to ceiling. She smiled and began choosing some books. Ten minutes later she had quite a high stack.

"Well, this should do for tonight," she said to Lumiere.

"Mon dieu!" Lumiere exclaimed. "You must be a speed-reader!" Then he noticed the grin on Belle's face. "Oh, I get it," he said sheepishly. "That's a joke."

Belle began to make her way across the polished floor. She clutched the teetering pile of books to her chest with one hand. Lumiere was in the other. Crash! The books scattered all over the marble floor. She placed Lumiere down and began to pick up the books. One

had slid across the room and was peeking out from underneath a bookshelf.

Lumiere hopped over to it. "It's stuck," he told Belle. She knelt on the floor and gave the book a sharp tug. Then she peered under the shelf. "I think there's something else under here," she said. She reached out and grabbed a dusty old book with a torn cover. She blew on it, sending the dust flying.

Lumiere sneezed.

"Bless you, Lumiere!" Belle said. "But look at this! I'll bet this has been under that bookshelf for quite a long time." There was a knight and a dragon on the cover. The knight had a terrified look on his face. Belle laughed and added it to her pile. She picked up Lumiere and carefully headed upstairs.

The hallway was dark and the shadows were spooky. But with the cheerful Lumiere as her guide, Belle was soon safely in her room.

Chapter Two

*B*elle sat on the edge of her bed wearing a soft nightgown with a pretty pink pattern. Lumiere perched on the night table beside the bed.

"Are you comfortable, mademoiselle?" the candelabrum asked.

Belle settled herself under the goose-down comforter. She plumped up the fluffy pillows behind her. "Why, yes," she said, "I feel like a princess!" She reached over to the pile of books next to the bed.

"Romance . . . adventure . . . fables . . . which shall I read first?" she wondered aloud. Then the dusty book on the top of the pile caught her eye. She picked it up, flipped open the cover, and began to read.

After a few minutes, Lumiere cleared his throat politely. "Ahem. I hate to be so bold, *ma chère*. But perhaps you could read . . . out loud?" he asked.

Belle smiled. "How silly of me, of course!" She was delighted that her new friend was interested in books, too!

She started again from the beginning: "Once upon a time, in a faraway land, there lived a handsome young knight named

William. He was kind and fair and had a very good sense of humour. He was nice to animals and small children, and he was well known for baking the finest four-and-twenty blackbird pie in the countryside. But there was just one problem. He was terrified of dragons! Even the sight of a small lizard would make him break out in a cold sweat. Luckily for him, he had never had to face one of the horrifying creatures. Then, one day, that all changed. . . ."

Belle giggled. What a fun story! How Chip would love it! Perhaps she would read it to him tomorrow at breakfast.

"Go on," said Lumiere, leaning forward.

Belle kept reading. "William was out on his horse, Midnight, looking for adventure.

It was a beautiful summer day, which quickly became a sticky, hot summer afternoon. William stopped to let his horse get a drink of water.

"As Midnight drank, William began eyeing the cool, clear water. Perhaps he would go for a quick swim to cool off. First, he took off his gloves, or gauntlets. Next, he removed his helmet and breastplate, and then struggled out of the rest. It was tiring work. Finally he was down to his long underwear when he heard a giggle.

"William dove behind a nearby bush. 'Who goes there?' he shouted.

"'It is I, Princess Isabella,' came the reply.

"The voice was very sweet and pretty. William peered around the bush. A beautiful

princess with long golden hair was standing there, her hands on her hips. She looked as if she was trying hard not to laugh. His face burned with embarrassment.

"'I beg your pardon, princess,' William said. 'If you would just hand me my armour, I would be very pleased to make your acquaintance.'

"The princess laughed as she gathered the

various pieces of William's suit of armour. When he was finally dressed, he stepped out from behind the bush and gave a deep bow. 'Sir William, at your service,' he said.

"William's breastplate was on backwards, but Princess Isabella was too polite to point that out. Instead, she thanked him for making her laugh. It had been a long time since she had smiled, she told him.

"'I am very glad to have brought you merriment,' said William. 'But why, pray tell, have you been so sad?'

"'A terrible dragon has been terrorizing my father's kingdom,' she explained. 'My father has promised my hand in marriage to the first knight who can defeat him. But Sir Halitosis is the only knight brave enough to take my father up on his challenge. And I don't like Sir Halitosis at all – he has breath worse than a fire-breathing dragon!'

"William felt his knees begin to knock together with fright. His worst fear! Yikes, he thought. But he smiled bravely and said, 'Dragon? Why, I eat dragons for breakfast!' Midnight snorted."

Belle took a deep breath. The handsome young knight was certainly in trouble! She turned to Lumiere. He was leaning forward so far he looked as if he was about to topple off the nightstand. "Shall I keep reading?" she teased. "Or perhaps it's time for bed?"

"No, no!" Lumiere cried. "Keep reading, s'il vous plaît! I am on the edge of my seat, er, I mean nightstand!"

Belle returned to the story: "Luckily, the princess was as smart and brave as she was beautiful. She paid a visit to a wizard who gave her a Cap of Invisibility for the knight to wear." Belle lowered her voice as she read. "'Good luck, my brave knight,' Princess Isabella said, holding up the small cap.

"Sir William put on a brave smile for his princess. He lowered his head, and Isabella placed the cap upon it. *Poof!* Just like that, he vanished.

"'William, are you there?' she asked worriedly.

"'Why, yes, I am, dear Isabella,' the young knight replied. 'I am sorry if I frightened you by disappearing like that.' He reached up and plucked the cap off his head. He immediately reappeared. 'Perhaps I should postpone this adventure and become visible again . . . ' His voice trailed off.

"'Tarry not, William,' replied Isabella. 'You have a dragon to defeat today.'

"William gulped. Unless she also had a Scarf of Silence for him to wear, that dragon was going to hear his knees knocking from a mile away. But he smiled bravely at Isabella.

"'I have faith in you, Sir William,' said Isabella. 'Now place that Cap of Invisibility back upon your head and slay that dragon!'

"William took a deep breath. He placed the cap on his head, and once more he vanished."

"Oh, my goodness!" cried a voice. "What will happen next?" Belle and Lumiere turned their heads. And there was Wardrobe, looking terribly anxious!

Belle laughed. "I didn't realize you were listening!" she called out.

"I'm on pins and needles!" cried Wardrobe.

"Well, let's find out what happens next," said Belle. Just then, she let out a loud yawn. "Excuse me," she said. Cogsworth the mantel clock may not have been there to tell her the time, but Belle knew that it was getting quite late. But she (and Lumiere and Wardrobe) just had to know how the story ended. Belle smiled and turned the page. . . .

She looked up, blinking in confusion. "That's it," she said. "There's nothing more."

"That can't possibly be the end," said Lumiere. He frowned. "Can it?"

Belle shook her head. "No, the last chapter must be missing. This is an old book. Perhaps the pages fell out." She closed the book. "We can check the library tomorrow. Maybe the last chapter is still under the bookshelf."

Wardrobe sighed. "I guess we have no choice. We'll have to wait to find out what happens," she said sadly. "Good night, Belle. Sweet dreams, Lumiere."

"Sweet dreams," said Lumiere.

"Good night, my friends," Belle said softly.

Lumiere put his hands together and snuffed out the candles. "Do you mind. . . ?" he asked Belle.

Belle realized that Lumiere could not blow out the candle on his head by himself. "Of course!" she said. And then the room was dark.

Belle lay in bed, her mind racing. What happened to the knight? Did he defeat the dragon? Did he win the love of his princess? Or did she have to marry the mean old knight with the bad breath?

"I'll never get to sleep!" Belle whispered to herself. But within moments her eyelids fluttered shut. And she was sound asleep.

Chapter Three

$\mathcal{E}$arly the next morning, there was a sharp knock on the bedroom door. Belle woke with a start. She was having a strange dream. She and her father were battling a dragon with the help of an invisible princess.

She yawned and stretched. Sunlight streamed through the windows, and the birds were singing. For a moment, she thought she was at home in her own bed. Then she realized with a pang that she was still a prisoner in the Beast's castle. But she wasn't sad for long. For she had just remembered that there was a missing chapter to find.

"Come in," she said, sitting up in bed.

The door swung open and Cogsworth stood in the doorway. He looked a little embarrassed to be disturbing Belle while she was still in her nightgown.

"I beg your pardon, mademoiselle," he said. "But breakfast is served in the dining room." As the head of the household, it was Cogworth's job to make sure that everything was running just as his master liked. And the master had been up early and already had his breakfast. He had seemed unhappy that Belle wasn't there to join him.

Cogsworth glared at Lumiere. The candelabrum was sound asleep. "Wake up, you lazy ball of wax!" he cried.

"Oh, please don't get angry with Lumiere," said Belle. "It's my fault, Cogsworth," she said in a soothing voice. "I kept him up late last night reading a book."

"What, what . . . " Lumiere leaped up and nearly fell off the bedside table. "Aah, good morning," he said pleasantly to Belle. He scowled at Cogsworth. "Interrupting my beauty sleep again, you overgrown pocket watch?"

"We'll be down in a moment," Belle told the mantel clock, trying to smooth things over between the two. Then she picked up the book on the nightstand.

"I do wonder if we'll ever find that missing chapter," she said out loud. Idly, she began to flip through the book.

Cogsworth was interested despite himself. The book in Belle's hands looked oddly familiar.

Belle noticed him staring. She held the book out. "Cogsworth, do you know anything about this book?" she asked.

Cogsworth walked into the room. "As if I have time for this nonsense," he muttered. "Breakfast is waiting!" But there was a twinkle of excitement in his eye.

"Why, bless my clock springs!" he exclaimed when he got a closer look at the book's cover. "That was the master's when he was a young lad." He shook his head. "But it has been missing for years!"

"What else can you tell us, Cogsworth?" asked Lumiere.

Cogsworth put his hands together, deep in thought. "All I remember is that the master's tutor asked him to read this book and write a report. And all the master wanted to do was play with his toy soldiers." He cleared his throat. "The master was a little, well, short-tempered at the time. Youth, you know."

Belle hid a small smile.

"So the master threw the book across the room and an entire section of it fell out," Cogsworth continued. "The tutor was disappointed and took the book – and the toy soldiers – away. My, was the master angry after that! That's all I remember. . . ."

He shook his head at the memory. "And here it is after all these years! Where on earth did you find it?"

"Under a bookshelf in the library!" Belle said. She opened the book to show him where the missing section was. To everyone's surprise, a slip of paper fell out and drifted to the floor. Cogsworth rushed over and picked it up. Lumiere hopped down from the table and tried to pull the paper out of Cogsworth's hands.

Belle watched in alarm. It looked as if they would rip it in two! "Excuse me!" Belle cried. "I'll take that!" She jumped out of bed and held out her hand. Lumiere let go, and Cogsworth fell to the ground. The mantel clock stood up, brushed himself off, and handed it over, a blush spreading over his clock face.

Belle smoothed out the paper and took a close look.

"I think it's a note!" she exclaimed. "Could it be a clue?"

"Read it, mademoiselle, read it!" begged Lumiere.

Belle read the note:

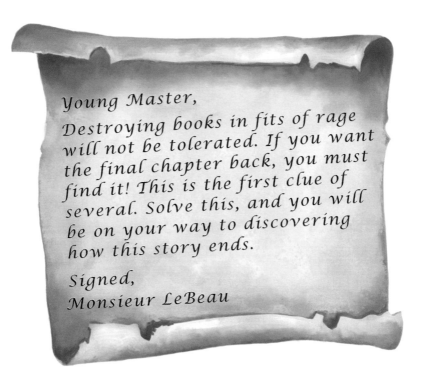

Young Master,

Destroying books in fits of rage will not be tolerated. If you want the final chapter back, you must find it! This is the first clue of several. Solve this, and you will be on your way to discovering how this story ends.

Signed,
Monsieur LeBeau

She flipped the note over. "The clue is written on the other side!" she said excitedly.

Cogsworth cleared his throat. "As head

of this household, may I suggest that we meet after breakfast to read the first clue? Mademoiselle, you need to eat. Lumiere and I must attend to a few household duties, then we will be ready to begin the search."

Lumiere sighed. "Party pooper," he said.

Belle smiled at Cogsworth. "I think Cogsworth is right. We'll all think better after a good breakfast," she said.

Cogsworth grinned. He liked it when he was right.

"I'll see you after breakfast," Belle said. "Then the search shall begin!"

Chapter Four

"Good morning, my dear!" Mrs Potts said cheerfully as Belle walked into the dining room. "A spot of tea for you?"

"Yes, thank you," said Belle. She sat at the table, unfolded a crisp white napkin and placed it on her lap. The note was in her apron pocket. Her fingers were itching to pull it out and read it, but she decided it was only fair to wait until everyone was together.

Chip hopped over, a big smile on his little face. "Good morning, Belle!" he cried.

"Good morning, Chip," said Belle. As she began to eat her breakfast, she told the little teacup and his mother about the mysterious book with the missing chapter.

Chip was wide-eyed. "A mystery!" he exclaimed. "How exciting! I am an excellent detective," he said, bragging. "Mama, can I help her? Can I? Can I?"

"If mademoiselle says it's all right," Mrs Potts told him. "But I don't want you getting in the way."

"I'd be honoured," said Belle. "I'm meeting Cogsworth and Lumiere after breakfast to read the first clue. Will you join us?"

Chip jumped up so high he spilled a little

tea on the tablecloth. But Mrs Potts was so pleased to see her son happy that she didn't say a word about it.

After breakfast, Mrs Potts tidied up. Lumiere, Cogsworth and Chip gathered on the table in front of Belle.

"This is very exciting, no?" asked Lumiere.

"Yes!" Chip said with a giggle.

Belle pulled out the paper, smoothed it on the table, and read it out loud:

To find this clue
you'll be hard put.
On a dark grey night,
It's underfoot.

Belle read the clue to herself again, then looked up slowly. "What could it mean?" she wondered.

The clock, the candelabrum and the small teacup with the chip all stared back at her blankly.

Cogsworth cleared his throat. "*Hmmm,*" he said. "This is more difficult than I had imagined!" The mantel clock paced back and forth. "Let's start at the beginning. A clue is hidden somewhere in this castle. It will lead us to another clue, and another until we find the missing book chapter."

He spun around and stared at everyone. "Are you with me so far?" he asked.

"Yes," Lumiere and Chip replied.

Belle nodded, hiding a smile. The mantel

clock was taking this hunt very seriously!

Cogsworth continued to pace. "We need to think of something that would be under your feet on a dark night," he said. "Any suggestions?"

"A rug?" suggested Chip.

"A rug!" Cogsworth repeated. He looked at Belle. "What do you think?"

"That's a good guess, Chip," Belle said.

"But a rug is always under your feet, whether it's night or day," she explained gently.

Cogsworth nodded. "As I thought. It is not a rug!"

"If it is a grey night, perhaps the clue is saying that it is raining!" exclaimed Lumiere. "Could it be . . . a doormat?"

Cogsworth scowled. "We don't have a doormat," he said, rolling his eyes at the candelabrum. "Have you ever seen a castle with a doormat?"

"Well, do you have a better idea?" Lumiere asked, poking him in the chest.

Belle stood up. "Maybe if we walked around the castle, we'd get an idea," she suggested.

Everyone thought that was a good plan.

They left the dining room and began to wander the halls of the castle.

They walked and walked. They passed by big statues, splendid paintings and beautiful tapestries. But nothing that would be underfoot. On any night, grey or otherwise.

"This is a very big castle," Belle said.

Finally the four came to a stop in the hall of armour. Dozens of suits of armour lined the walls on both sides.

Belle sighed. "I feel like the clue is so close!" she cried. "Like it is right under our noses!"

The three nodded in agreement. The only question was – where?

Little Chip glanced around the hallway. He loved looking at the suits of armour, imagining the brave knights who must have worn them long ago.

Suddenly he realized something. "Hey!" he shouted. "These knights look pretty dark grey to me!"

"Chip, that's it!" Belle cried. "You did it!"

"And if the clue is underfoot..." Cogsworth began.

"Then the clue must be under the feet of one of the suits of armour!" finished Lumiere. "Let's start looking!"

Belle knelt in front of the first suit of armour and ran her hand underneath one of the feet. To her surprise, the suit of armour began to shake and quiver. She drew back her hand in alarm. "What's going on?" she asked.

"Enchanted as well," said Cogsworth with a shrug. "And ticklish, too, it looks like!"

They went up one side of the hallway, peering under the feet of each suit of armour. But there wasn't a clue to be found. Next, they began searching those on the other side. Finally, they reached the very last suit of armour. They looked at each other.

"This is it," said Belle. "It's got to be here!" She felt under the left foot. The ticklish suit of armour began to shake, squeaking away.

"*Hmmm*, needs oil," said Cogsworth. He never forgot his head-of-household duties.

Belle took a deep breath. Then she reached under the right foot. And there it was! She held it up.

"Hooray!" shouted Chip.

"We did it!" said Cogsworth.

"What does it say?" Lumiere wanted to know.

Belle read:

> It's big. It's grand.
> For all to see.
> You'll find it under
> number seventy-three.

Everyone stared.

"Huh?" said Chip.

Belle patted the little cup. She knew exactly how he felt – totally confused.

Chapter Five

The four wandered over to a nearby couch. Belle, Chip and Lumiere sank into the cushions in silence. Cogsworth paced back and forth in front of them.

"This is harder than I thought," said Lumiere.

"The clues are very . . . mysterious," Belle agreed.

"Stop pacing, Cogsworth!" cried Lumiere. "You are making me nervous!"

Cogsworth glared at the candelabrum. "It's how I do my best thinking!" he explained.

"Then do your thinking somewhere else," said Lumiere.

Belle shook her head. Those two were always arguing!

"I have a guess," said Lumiere. "I am not sure if it is correct. But the number seventy-three made me start thinking. However, I could be wrong. . . ."

"Out with it, Lumiere!" Cogsworth sputtered. "We haven't got all day!"

Belle hid a smile. Actually, they did have all day. And the next day, too. The mystery was a decade old, for goodness' sake! But she understood the mantel clock's impatience.

"Please tell us, Lumiere," she said.

"I was thinking that perhaps it is the grand piano," the candelabrum replied.

Cogsworth wanted to argue. But it was as good a guess as any. "That could be it," he said, nodding. "A piano has eighty-eight keys, so it could be under the seventy-third!"

"Exactly my thoughts!" replied Lumiere.

He and Cogsworth looked at each other in surprise. They had just agreed on something!

"To the conservatory!" shouted Chip.

Belle followed the three household objects down several hallways and into another wing of the castle. And there, in the conservatory, stood a beautiful grand piano. They all stared at it. Could this be where the next clue was hidden?

Belle stepped forward, counted the keys, and touched the seventy-third one. It made a plinking sound.

"Still in tune after all these years!" said Cogsworth proudly.

Belle truly wanted Lumiere to be right. But it just didn't seem possible. "I just don't see where a clue could be hidden," she said slowly.

"Maybe it's inside!" cried Chip. And before anyone could stop him, he climbed right inside the top of the piano. They could hear him hopping around.

"Nothing!" he said, poking his head out.

As if on cue, they each let out a loud sigh. This made them all laugh.

"What else is 'grand' around here?" Lumiere asked.

Belle grinned. "Everything!" she said, thinking about the humble cottage where she lived with her father. Their entire house would probably fit in the front hall! The grand staircase alone was bigger than . . .

"That's it!" she shouted.

"What's it?" squeaked Chip.

"The grand staircase!" Belle said proudly.

Cogsworth and Lumiere broke out into huge smiles. "Under step number seventy-three," Cogsworth said, nodding his head. "Belle, you're a genius!"

" . . . seventy-one . . . seventy-two . . . seventy-three!" they counted together. They all looked at each other. It was almost too exciting!

"Belle, will you do the honours?" asked Cogsworth. Belle slipped her hand between the step and the velvety rug. And there, waiting for them, was clue number three.

She sat on the step, and the others gathered around her. She read aloud:

> Where is the next clue?
> It's found within
> Two brothers
> Who were very grim.

Lumiere looked puzzled. "So we must find two unhappy brothers?" he asked. This didn't sound easy at all.

"Those two peddlers from the village were always rather cross," said Cogsworth. "They looked a lot alike, too," he said. "Lumiere, do you think they were related?"

"Hard to tell," answered Lumiere. "Besides, how would we find them after all these years?"

"We will hunt them down!" Cogsworth said. "Search every home in the village until we find them . . ."

Chip leaned over and whispered to Belle. "I think they're wrong," he said.

"I think you're right," Belle whispered back. The clue sounded so familiar to her. Two brothers who were very grim . . . two grim brothers . . . "The Brothers Grimm!" she said out loud.

Chip grinned. Cogsworth and Lumiere stopped talking and looked at Belle in confusion.

"The Brothers Grimm were two German brothers who collected fairy tales and published them in books," she explained. But they still looked puzzled. "To the library!" she said. "The clue is in one of their fairy-tale collections!"

Just then Mrs Potts appeared at the foot of the stairs. "Tut-tut," she said. "No one is going anywhere until you have had a nice lunch. This chapter has been missing for more than eleven years; an extra hour isn't going to change anything. We're serving beef stew!"

Belle wanted to argue, but a sudden rumbling in her stomach stopped her. They'd been so busy searching for clues that she hadn't realized it was lunchtime already. Suddenly she could smell the rich aroma of beef stew and freshly baked bread. It smelled heavenly.

"Time for lunch!" she agreed.

Belle made her way to the dining room. She was surprised that the table was set for one. "Will anyone be joining me for lunch?" she asked.

Mrs Potts couldn't seem to look Belle directly in the eye. "The master has decided to take his lunch in his quarters," she said.

Belle shrugged sadly, placed her napkin on her lap and dug in. The stew was delicious.

Word of the treasure hunt had spread among the enchanted household objects. So by the time Belle had finished eating, quite a crowd had gathered in the dining room. They were all eager to join the hunt. Belle, Cogsworth, Chip and Lumiere led the group down the halls to the library to find the next clue. They chattered excitedly as they walked.

Belle pushed open the doors to the library and walked inside. The enchanted objects filled the room behind her.

Belle addressed the crowd. "We are looking for the fourth clue," she explained. "And we know that it is hidden inside a book written by the Brothers Grimm. Now all we have to do is find that book!"

Everyone looked around the room. There were thousands of books on the shelves. The shelves rose high above their heads.

"It's like looking for a needle in a haystack!" someone called out.

Belle held up her hand. "Not exactly," she said. She had spent some time exploring the library since the Beast had presented it to her. "There is a section for each subject," she told the crowd. "And we're looking for a book of fairy tales."

"Where is the fairy-tale section?" Babette, the maid who was a feather duster, wanted to know.

Belle smiled and pointed to one of the very highest shelves. "Unfortunately, fairy tales and folklore is up there," she said.

The crowd gasped. Surely mademoiselle would not climb so high!

They all watched in disbelief as Belle walked toward a nearby ladder and began to climb. Up, up, up.

"I can't watch," said Wardrobe, closing her eyes. But she opened them again an instant later. "But I can't not watch, either!"

"Be careful, my dear!" shouted Mrs Potts. She looked around. "Has anyone seen Chip?"

"I'm up here, Mama!" cried the little teacup, popping his head out of Belle's apron pocket.

"Chip!" said Belle. "What are you doing?"

"I don't want to miss anything!" Chip explained. "This is the most fun I've had in . . . forever!"

"Chip, be careful!" Mrs Potts cried.

Belle gripped the rungs even more tightly as she climbed higher and higher. Finally, she reached the top. Now she had to find the right book. She didn't want to have to make that climb again anytime soon! There was one leather-bound volume by the Brothers Grimm – *Children's and Household Tales*. She tucked the

book into her apron and began to descend.

She stepped down off the ladder and turned to face the crowd. She was flushed and a bit out of breath. A stray piece of hair had escaped from her ponytail. She tucked it behind her ear.

There was silence as the objects stared at her. Finally Wardrobe said, "I can hardly contain myself. What does it say?"

Belle pulled the book out of her apron pocket. She flipped through the pages. She held the book upside down and shook it. She bit her lip. "There is no clue," she said. "It must have been lost after all these years. I'm so sorry." She hung her head sadly.

Chapter Six

"*O*hhhhhhh," groaned the household objects. They had been so excited. And it was all over as soon as it had started.

"Don't be sad!" a little voice piped up. "There is a clue!" Chip poked his head out of Belle's apron pocket. "It's here in your pocket. It must have fallen out while you were climbing down!"

"*Yay!*" everyone cheered.

Belle was so happy! She reached into her pocket, set Chip on the floor with a little pat, and pulled out the note. She read:

The final clue
You're almost home.
You'll find it
Underneath the gnome.

"Underneath the gnome?" a voice called out. "Belle, is that a joke?"

Belle shook her head. "No, that's exactly what it says," she said. "Gnome."

"Maybe there is a gnome hidden in the forest tapestry!" Babette exclaimed.

"What a wonderful idea!" said Lumiere.

"There are many creatures in that tapestry."

The group marched to a long hallway. They stood before the forest tapestry and studied it carefully. Belle made her way to the front of the crowd and looked at it for herself. There were trees, mountains, plants, flowers and animals woven into the fabric. But not a single gnome – or other magical creature – to be found.

"What about that painting of the field of flowers in the drawing room?" Mrs Potts suggested. "Surely there could be a gnome hidden there!"

They rushed to the drawing room as fast as they could. "I see it!" someone called. But on closer examination, it turned out to be a toadstool with a red cap.

The group was slowly getting smaller. Wardrobe had wandered back upstairs to air out her closets. Babette noticed some dust in the drawing room and stayed behind to tidy up. Mrs Potts gathered the bowls and plates and started to herd them back into the dining room.

"Believe it or not, it's time to start getting ready for dinner," she explained. "Sorry Belle, sorry Chip. Maybe after a nice meal and a good night's sleep . . ." Her voice trailed off. "Well, we'll figure it out tomorrow."

One by one the household objects got back to work. Soon Belle, Lumiere, Cogsworth and little Chip were the only ones left.

"What is a gnome anyway?" Chip wanted to know.

"Gnomes are tiny creatures with long white beards and pointy hats," Belle explained. "Some people believe they really exist, but the only ones I've ever seen have been statues in people's gardens."

"That's it!" cried Cogsworth. "In the garden! How silly of us!"

The four friends went outside. The gardens had become rather overgrown throughout the years, which made the search difficult.

Belle crawled out from underneath a large bush. She had leaves in her hair. "Not there, either," she said. They were out of places to look.

"Can I help you?" a voice asked. They spun around. It was the old gardener, who had been turned into a watering can. They explained the story to him.

He chuckled and shook his head. "These were always very formal gardens," he said. "We never had any gnome statues." He wrinkled his brow in thought. "But come to think of it, it does sound kind of familiar."

"Really?" said Belle.

"Yes," he answered. "I remember the young master talking about a gnome. Or was it an elf?" He sighed. "Too long ago to remember . . ." The gardener returned to the greenhouse, shaking his head sadly.

Belle's shoulders drooped as the four made their way back into the castle. Once

the door was shut behind them, Belle turned to the others. "That's it!" she said. "We'll ask the Beast!"

Lumiere and Cogsworth looked at each other in alarm. "No, no, no!" cried Cogsworth. "That is a very bad idea!"

Lumiere put his hands on his hips.

"Mademoiselle, I must discourage this!"

Neither he nor Cogsworth wanted anything to happen that might make the Beast angry again. They were counting on the two to fall in love and break the spell!

But Chip had no idea about any of this. "Yes, Belle, yes!" he shouted. "He will know. And then we can find the missing chapter!"

Before Cogsworth's and Lumiere's unbelieving eyes, Belle marched right up the stairs to the Beast's quarters.

"Perhaps the master will be in a good mood," Lumiere said hopefully.

"Perhaps," said Cogsworth. "But highly unlikely!"

Chapter Seven

$\mathcal{B}$elle knocked on the Beast's door. She had been full of excitement as she climbed the stairs. Now, she suddenly felt nervous. "Don't be silly, Belle," she said out loud. "Why wouldn't he want to help you? It's his mystery anyway!"

There was no answer. She took a deep breath for courage and opened the door. The Beast's bedroom was surprisingly neat.

She tiptoed inside. The Beast was sitting in a chair, staring gloomily out the window.

"Excuse me," Belle started to say. "But . . ."

"Oh, there you are!" he growled. "You don't even show up for breakfast. And then you trespass in my private quarters?"

"I'm sorry," Belle said. "I thought maybe you hadn't heard my knock."

"I heard it," said the Beast. "I was just ignoring it. Hoping whoever it was would go away."

Lumiere and Cogsworth were listening outside the door. They looked at each other. This could not be going any worse!

"Is there anything you need?" the Beast asked gruffly.

"No," replied Belle. "Everything is fine."

"Then I will see you at dinner," said the Beast, turning back to the window.

"But . . ." Belle started to say.

"Enough!" shouted the Beast. He stomped across the room.

"But we found a note from Monsieur LeBeau!" Belle called. "He left some clues for you! We need your help!"

Without a backward glance, the Beast threw open the door and raced down the stairs.

Shaking her head, Belle left the room. In the hallway she found Lumiere, Cogsworth, and Chip, all looking dazed.

Sadly, the four wandered downstairs. Without the Beast's help, the treasure hunt

was officially over. Mrs Potts saw their long faces and suggested they make themselves comfortable in front of the fire in the sitting room.

They sat in silence, each thinking their own thoughts. Lumiere and Cogsworth were worried. It seemed as if the Beast and Belle were back to square one – and time was running out. Mrs Potts was thinking the same thing, but she was also wondering if the plates and utensils were arranging themselves nicely on the table, or if she would have to go in and supervise. Chip was sad because the fun was over. Things had sure gotten exciting since Belle showed up!

"I know I shouldn't have gone into his room uninvited," Belle said. "But he didn't need to be such a . . . beast!"

"I know," said a deep voice. They all spun around. There stood the Beast, his head bowed in embarrassment.

"I was very rude, and I apologize," the Beast said. "I was just disappointed that you didn't show up for breakfast," he said. "And I was sulking in my room. I didn't even listen to what you had to tell me. Did I really hear you say something about my old tutor, Monsieur LeBeau?"

Belle stood up. And then she raced out of the room.

The Beast's eyes widened. "She is so angry with me!" he cried. "How will I make it up to her?" He sank into a large chair, his head in his paws.

"Build her another library?" joked Lumiere.

Cogsworth, Mrs Potts and even Chip glared at him.

"Sorry," said Lumiere sheepishly.

But moments later, Belle was back, out of breath. She knelt beside the Beast's chair and placed the book in his paws. "Does this look familiar?" she asked gently.

"*The Knight Who Was Afraid of Dragons!*" the Beast cried. "I searched and searched – "

"I found it under one of the bookshelves in the library," Belle explained.

The Beast was deep in thoughts of the past. "Monsieur LeBeau told me I had to read the whole book and write a report. But I wanted to play with my toy soldiers. So I threw the book against the wall, and the last chapter fell out. Soon after, Monsieur LeBeau had to leave unexpectedly to take care of some family matters. He asked me to try again, and told me he had hidden the book under a desk in the library for me to find. But when I looked, it was gone. I felt terrible about the way I treated my tutor. I thought if I found the book and did the report, I could somehow make it up to him." He shook his head sadly. "And then I never saw Monsieur LeBeau again."

"Someone must have accidentally kicked the book under the shelf!" Belle exclaimed. "And there it's been for years and years!"

"I can't believe it!" said the Beast.

Belle smiled at him. "Monsieur LeBeau left you a series of clues that lead to the missing chapter!" she told him.

The Beast stared at her. "He did?"

Chip jumped up excitedly. "And now we're up to clue number . . . "

Belle held up a hand. "I have a great idea! Why don't we re-create the treasure hunt for you," she told the Beast. "Just as Monsieur LeBeau would have wanted it."

The Beast paced back and forth in the drawing room as Belle and her friends replaced all the clues. Then she handed him the first one.

The Beast found the first two clues fairly quickly. But the Brothers Grimm clue took him quite a while. (He ended up needing some help from Belle.) He climbed up the ladder and retrieved the book.

The final clue was now in the Beast's hands. They watched him carefully as he read it. Then he frowned.

Belle's heart sank. Had the trail truly come to a dead end?

Chapter Eight

The Beast put a paw over his eyes.

"I'm sorry," said Belle. "It has been such a long time. It was silly of me to think that you'd remember after all these years."

"Of course I remember!" said the Beast. "Monsieur LeBeau was always trying to make learning fun for me. He remembered my favourite place to hide." He smiled. "Whenever I didn't want to study, I would run and hide in the middle of the hedge maze. I would lie in the grass and watch the clouds go by . . . next to a rock that looked just like a gnome! Monsieur LeBeau would leave me alone for a while. And then he'd find me. And after we both watched the clouds together, we'd get back to work."

"He sounds like a wonderful tutor," said Belle.

"He was," said the Beast. "And I acted like such a spoiled boy around him." He sighed.

Belle took the Beast's paw. He showed her the way to the hedge maze.

"I've read about hedge mazes," said Belle as they stepped inside. "But I've never actually been in one before. How fun!"

They came to the first break in the hedges.

"Which way do we go?" Belle asked.

The Beast thought for a moment. "Left, definitely left," he said. It went this way for several more turns. The Beast did make one wrong turn, but he quickly discovered his mistake. In no time, they were in the centre of the maze.

Belle immediately sat down in the grass.

"Belle, what are you doing?" the Beast asked.

She motioned for him to join her. "I'm looking at the clouds!" she said. "Just like you used to!"

The Beast sat down beside her, and the two watched the clouds float by. But before long, they stood up. They were both too excited about finding the last clue.

"There he is!" said the Beast. He pointed to a tallish rock. Belle squinted. When you looked at it the right way, it did kind of look like a gnome, pointy hat and all.

"Oh, dear. We forgot to bring a shovel!" she cried.

But the Beast laughed. "Look at these claws!" he said, holding up his paws. "Who needs a shovel?"

Belle watched as the Beast began digging in the earth. Soon there was a large pile of dirt. But still no treasure.

"Monsieur LeBeau took his treasure hiding seriously!" said Belle.

The Beast nodded. "He took everything seriously. But he also made learning a lot of fun."

The Beast started digging again. Suddenly his expression changed. A huge smile broke out on his furry face. "Belle, I've found it!"

Belle held her breath as he pulled a tin box out of the ground. He stared at it. "After all these years," he said.

Belle could hardly stand the suspense. "Oh, please, open it!" she cried.

Slowly, the Beast unlatched the lid. Inside was the missing chapter. It was slightly damp, but in surprisingly good condition. Then he pulled out a tin soldier. "I can't believe it! My favourite soldier!" he cried. "I thought I lost it long ago!"

The Beast picked up an envelope and tore it open. "It's a note," he said quietly. He pulled it out and began to read aloud:

Young master,

Good work! You solved all
the clues and saw this through.
We may have our differences,
but I can see in you the fine,
outstanding man you will become.
I am so proud of you today.

Your humble tutor,
Monsieur LeBeau

Belle heard a muffled sob. Was the Beast
crying? Then she turned to discover that
all the household objects had followed
them into the maze. There wasn't a dry eye
among them!

"It's so beautiful!" said Mrs Potts. "I think there's something there that wasn't there before," she said to Lumiere.

"Yes!" he whispered. "The enchantment may be broken yet!"

"What?" asked Chip. "I don't get it!"

"Never you mind," said Mrs Potts. "Come on, everyone, time for dinner."

And after a delicious dinner (complete with singing and dancing plates, of course), Belle invited the Beast and all the household objects to the sitting room. In front of a roaring fire, she read the entire book out loud to the Beast and his staff. They laughed at the funny places, gasped at the surprising spots, and cheered at the end.

For yes, it had a happy ending. Wouldn't

you know it, the knight defeated the dragon,
the kingdom was returned to normal, and
the princess was able to marry the man she
loved. And they lived happily ever after.

And Belle and the Beast? Well, that's a
story for another time!

Don't miss the next enchanting Disney Princess chapter book!

Cinderella
The
Great Mouse
Mistake

One day, Gus the mouse decides to pick some beautiful roses for his dear friend Cinderelly. But when the evil Lady Tremaine finds out that the roses are from her garden, she gets very upset. Gus doesn't want Cinderella to get in trouble, so the two of them go to town to look for a new rosebush. Things go from bad to worse when Gus accidentally knocks over a cake that belongs to the king. The trouble is piling up – how will Gus and Cinderella ever get out of it?